See
Pip
Point

For Carole and Zane

SIMON SPOTLIGHT
An imprint of Simon & Schuster Children's Publishing Division
1230 Avenue of the Americas, New York, New York 10020
This Simon Spotlight edition May 2016
Copyright © 2003 by David Milgrim
SIMON SPOTLIGHT, READY-TO-READ, and colophon are registered trademarks of
Simon & Schuster, Inc.
For information about special discounts for bulk purchases, please contact
Simon & Schuster Special Sales at 1-866-506-1949
or business@simonandschuster.com.
Manufactured in the United States of America 0416 LAK
2 4 6 8 10 9 7 5 3 1
This book has been cataloged with the Library of Congress.
ISBN 978-1-4814-6785-8 (hc)
ISBN 978-1-4814-6784-1 (pbk)
ISBN 978-1-4814-6786-5 (eBook)

The adventures of otto

See Pip Point

David Milgrim

Ready-to-Read

Simon Spotlight

New York   London   Toronto   Sydney   New Delhi

See Pip.
See Pip point.

Point, point, point.
Point, point, point.
Point, point, point.

See Otto share.

Thank you,
Otto.

Oops,
there goes Pip.

See Pip go.

Go, go, go.

Uh-oh.

See Pip go up.
See Pip go way up.
See Pip go up, up,
and away.

See Zee the Bee.
See Zee the Bee fly.
See Zee the Bee fly
in his sleep.

Look out, Zee!

See Pip go down.
See Pip go way down.
See Pip go down,
   down to the ground.

Look! Here comes Otto!
Hurry, Otto, hurry!

See Otto save Pip!
Thank you, Otto!

Uh-oh.

See Otto and Pip crash.

See Otto and Pip splash.

Oops.

See Pip point.